I wish I could...
Walk with the
DINOSAURS

Written by Gordy Slack
Illustrated by C. Buck Reynolds

Dr. Peter Rodda, scientific advisor

CALIFORNIA ACADEMY OF SCIENCES

in cooperation with Roberts Rinehart Publishers

Acknowledgments
Thanks to Jerry Kay, Linda Allison and William S. Wells,
whose 1987 book, *Dinosaurs*, in the Academy's Science In Action Learning Series,
served as the springboard for this book.

International Standard Book Number 1-57098-117-5
Library of Congress Catalog Card Number 96-072306

Cover and book design by Archetype, Inc., Denver, Colorado

Published by Roberts Rinehart Publishers
5455 Spine Road
Boulder, Colorado 80301
303.530.4400

In cooperation with the California Academy of Sciences
Golden Gate Park
San Francisco, California 94118

Published in the UK and Ireland by
Roberts Rinehart Publishers
Trinity House, Charleston Road
Dublin 6, Ireland

Distributed to the trade by Publishers Group West

Manufactured in Hong Kong

Walk with the
DINOSAURS

I sure wish I could
walk with the dinosaurs.

You can, if you've got about 180 million years to spare.

Why so long?

- Earth is about four and a half billion years old.
- The first life forms appeared about three and a half billion years ago. They were microscopic bacteria-like creatures, so they left very little for scientists to study.
- The first vertebrates (animals with backbones) were fish-like. They appeared about 500 million years ago. Because bone is hard, they made good fossils.
- The first known reptile, *Westlothiana*, appeared about 363 million years ago.
- The first dinosaurs date to about 230 million years ago.

The Age of Dinosaurs lasted about
180 million years. But it ended about
65 million years ago. It's not easy
studying something that old.

Let's go have a look.

Paleontology Department

The Earth's history is broken into periods based on the kinds of animals that existed during those times. Including the present period, called the Quaternary, there are 12 periods. Three of these, the Triassic, the Jurassic, and the Cretaceous, are known as the Age of Dinosaurs because dinosaurs flourished during those periods.

Most dinosaurs became extinct at the end of the Cretaceous Period, 65 million years ago. That's a long time before humans arrived on the scene. The earliest humans didn't appear until more than 62 million years later—about two and a half million years ago.

Triassic Period
243–208 million

By the Triassic Period, reptiles had developed
into many different forms. Some of these were very big.
The Late Triassic marks the beginning of the
Age of Dinosaurs. Then, there was only one big continent,
called Pangaea. It was mostly covered with deserts.

Jurassic Period
208–146 million

Pangaea began to break up and shallow seas began
to spread across its surface. Huge meat-eating dinosaurs and
herbivores roamed the land.

Cretaceous Period
146–65 million

Great forests grew across the continents,
which had spread apart from one another. The Age of Dinosaurs
came to an abrupt end about 65 million years ago.

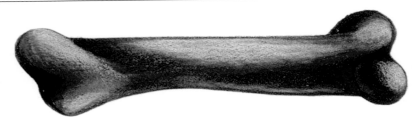

The word "paleo" means old, and paleontologists are scientists who study fossils to learn about life of the past, including dinosaurs. They hunt for fossils, clean them off, and then study them. It is amazing how much paleontologists have figured out from fossilized bones. Especially since the bones are usually broken and are hardly ever found in complete sets.

Believe it or not,
this hunk of rock will be a
Triceratops skull when
we're done with it.

When paleontologists find a dinosaur skeleton they dig it out of the ground very carefully. They sometimes use dental tools and brushes to separate fossils from the surrounding rock.

Paleontologists also study the layers of rock around the fossils. They are searching for clues about how and when the animals lived and died. The right interpretation is not always easy to make.

This fossil included both eggs in a nest and an adult dinosaur skeleton.

Was the dinosaur stealing the eggs?

Or was it caring for them?

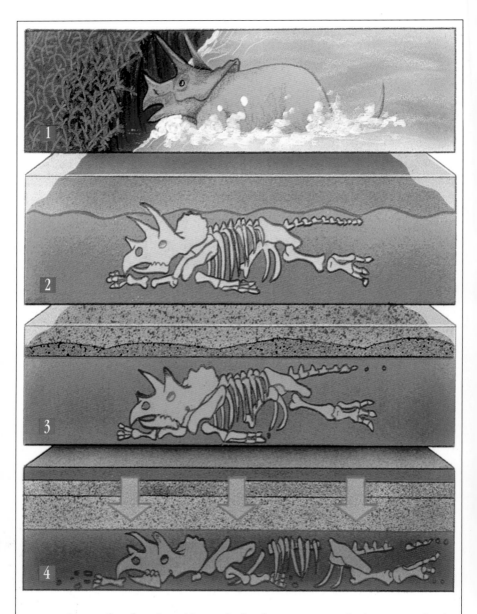

Fossils are often found in old river beds. If a *Triceratops*, say, died on a river bank, it might have become a fossil. It could have been buried by mud and sand as its flesh rotted. More layers of sediment could have piled up, turning the lower layers into rock. The bones would have been replaced by minerals from the surrounding rock that seeped into the bony structure.

Bones are not the only things that make fossils.
Even a footprint or something as soft as a feather can
make a fossil if the conditions are right.

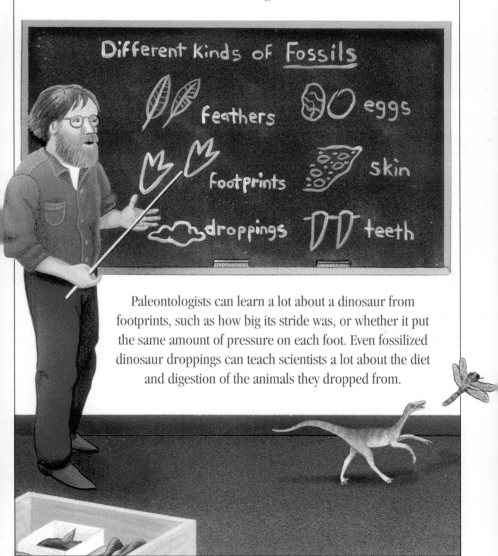

Paleontologists can learn a lot about a dinosaur from
footprints, such as how big its stride was, or whether it put
the same amount of pressure on each foot. Even fossilized
dinosaur droppings can teach scientists a lot about the diet
and digestion of the animals they dropped from.

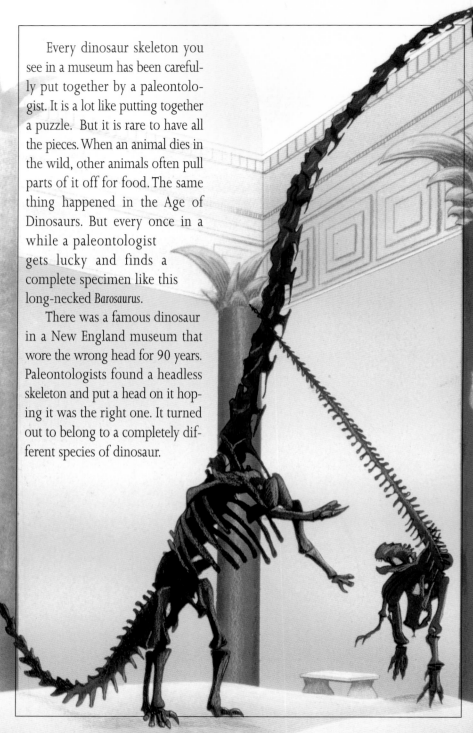

Every dinosaur skeleton you see in a museum has been carefully put together by a paleontologist. It is a lot like putting together a puzzle. But it is rare to have all the pieces. When an animal dies in the wild, other animals often pull parts of it off for food. The same thing happened in the Age of Dinosaurs. But every once in a while a paleontologist gets lucky and finds a complete specimen like this long-necked *Barosaurus*.

There was a famous dinosaur in a New England museum that wore the wrong head for 90 years. Paleontologists found a headless skeleton and put a head on it hoping it was the right one. It turned out to belong to a completely different species of dinosaur.

It takes a little imagination to get from fossils to realistic dinosaurs. But when you think about dinosaurs as much as I do, they start to seem alive. Take the *Deinonychus*, for example. By studying them very closely and making a few guesses, we were able to make these models.

I swear
I saw that claw
move!

They sure
look realistic.

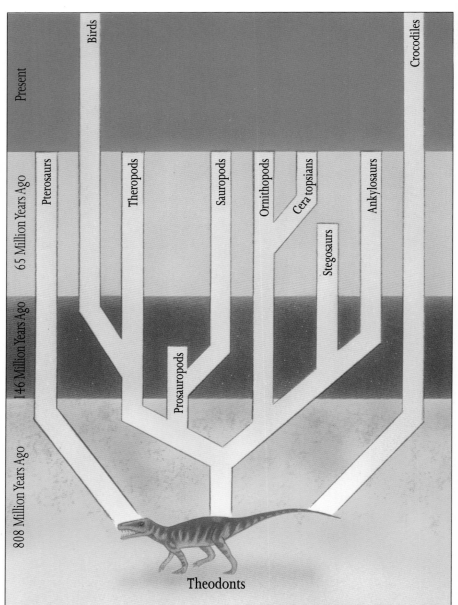

Present

65 Million Years Ago

146 Million Years Ago

808 Million Years Ago

Birds

Crocodiles

Pterosaurs

Theropods

Sauropods

Ornithopods

Cera topsians

Ankylosaurs

Stegosaurs

Prosauropods

Theodonts

In the Triassic Period there was a group of crocodile-like reptiles called theodonts. Many different kinds of animals evolved from them, including all of the dinosaurs and animals whose descendants became modern crocodiles and birds.

During the Triassic all of Earth's continents were attached in one huge landmass called Pangaea.

In the Late Triassic Period, between 220 and 230 million years ago, the first dinosaurs appeared. They were mostly small, agile hunters such as *Coelophysis*, which hunted in packs. Paleontologists say they probably ate each other as well as large reptiles.

At about that same time the *Plateosaurus* evolved in what is now Europe. *Plateosaurus* was the first really big dinosaur and grew to be about 26 feet long. It could stand on its hind feet and stretch out its long neck to reach vegetation growing high in the trees.

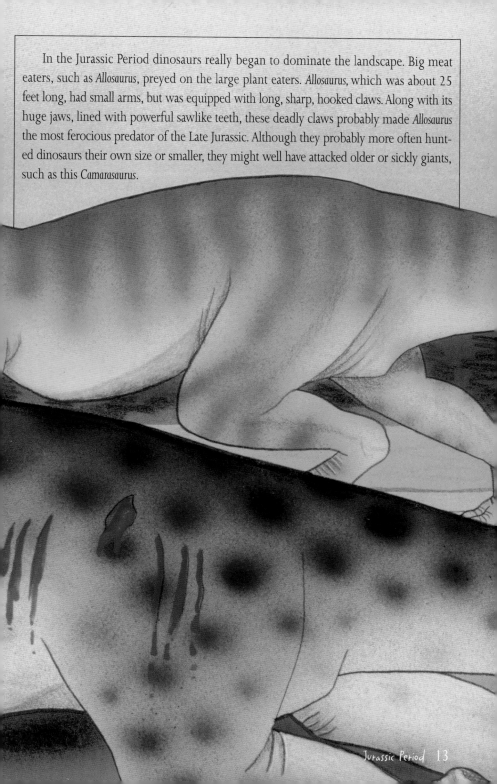

In the Jurassic Period dinosaurs really began to dominate the landscape. Big meat eaters, such as *Allosaurus*, preyed on the large plant eaters. *Allosaurus*, which was about 25 feet long, had small arms, but was equipped with long, sharp, hooked claws. Along with its huge jaws, lined with powerful sawlike teeth, these deadly claws probably made *Allosaurus* the most ferocious predator of the Late Jurassic. Although they probably more often hunted dinosaurs their own size or smaller, they might well have attacked older or sickly giants, such as this *Camarasaurus*.

By the Cretaceous Period, Pangaea had broken up and the separate continents looked something like those we know today. Since different populations of dinosaurs were then kept from each other by seas, they evolved in different ways. This helps explain why more dinosaurs lived in the Cretaceous than at any other time.

Hypsilophodon lived in the Mid-Cretaceous Period, about 120 million years ago. Because scientists have found *Hypsilophodon* fossils in groups, they think these dinosaurs traveled in herds. Some probably grazed while others kept a a sharp eye out for predators. *Hypsilophodon* had no armor, defensive teeth, or claws, but it could probably run faster than almost any other dinosaur we know of. Alertness and speed were the secrets to its success.

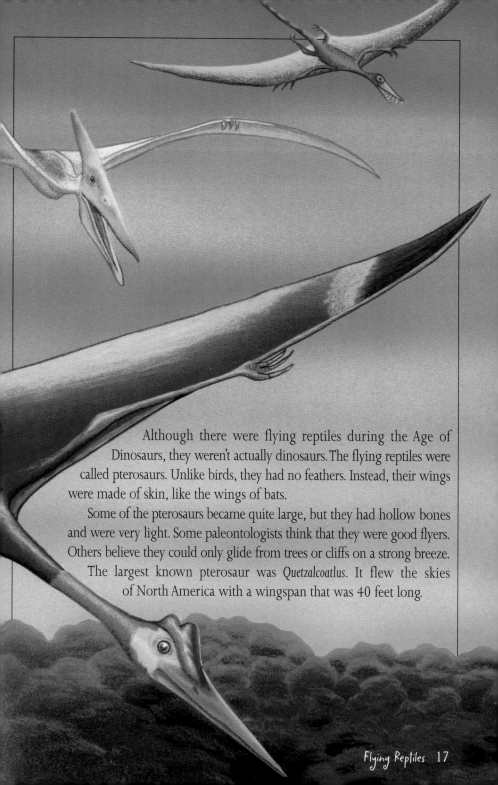

Although there were flying reptiles during the Age of Dinosaurs, they weren't actually dinosaurs. The flying reptiles were called pterosaurs. Unlike birds, they had no feathers. Instead, their wings were made of skin, like the wings of bats.

Some of the pterosaurs became quite large, but they had hollow bones and were very light. Some paleontologists think that they were good flyers. Others believe they could only glide from trees or cliffs on a strong breeze.

The largest known pterosaur was *Quetzalcoatlus*. It flew the skies of North America with a wingspan that was 40 feet long.

There also were large water
dwelling reptiles. The two best known
were *Plesiosaurus* and the smaller *Ichthyosaurus*.
They weren't dinosaurs either. There were no marine dinosaurs. But the water-dwelling reptiles did go extinct at the
same time as the dinosaurs.

When the winged reptiles, the pterosaurs, became
extinct, their place in the ecosystem was taken up by winged
mammals (bats). After the ichthyosaurs died out, they were
replaced by the swimming mammals (whales).

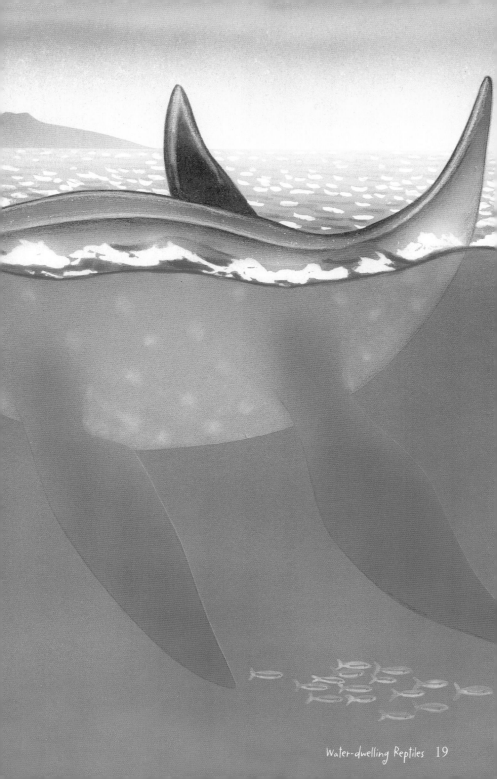

All living things change a little bit from one generation to the next. Over many generations these small changes add up to big ones. If a dinosaur changed in a way that allowed it to get more food, say, or to protect itself, then its chances of surviving and reproducing improved. When it reproduced, that helpful trait would have been passed on to its offspring. This process is called "natural selection."

If two populations of the same kind of dinosaur were separated (say mountains rose between them) they would probably change in different ways. One might get a long neck allowing it to reach food at the tops of trees. The other one might get powerful jaws allowing it to eat other dinosaurs. This is one important way that "new" dinosaurs evolved. But this kind of change was gradual and took a long, long time.

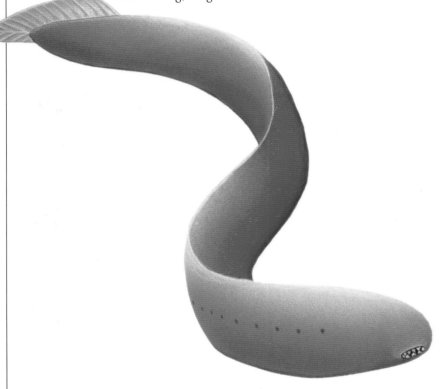

Through natural selection dinosaurs, mammals, and other vertebrates evolved from worm-like creatures called conodonts, which filled the seas between 570 and 510 million years ago.

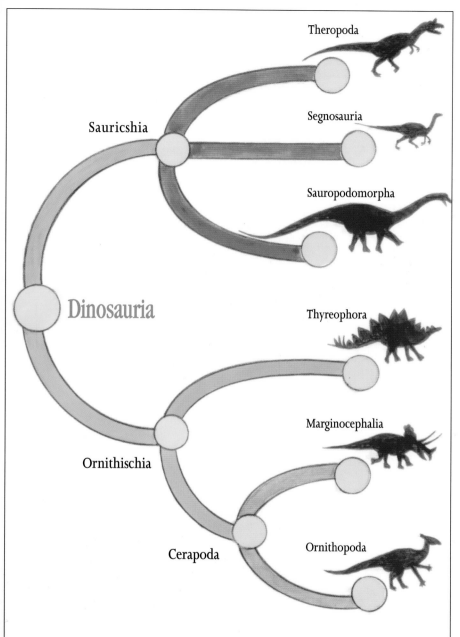

Theropoda

Segnosauria

Sauropodomorpha

Sauricshia

Dinosauria

Thyreophora

Marginocephalia

Ornithischia

Ornithopoda

Cerapoda

There are two main branches of the dinosaur family. Each of these divides further into three main groups. Each of the six groups includes many different species of dinosaur.

The Late Jurassic was the Age of Giants. Some dinosaurs had evolved into enormous creatures. Sauropods, long-necked herbivores, were the largest land animals that ever lived. And *Seismosaurus* was probably the largest sauropod. It was about 130 feet long and weighed as much as 100 tons. Its sheer size helped ward off predators.

Bigger dinosaurs can reach higher into trees to get choice leaves. But they also have to eat more food. A modern elephant eats about 300 pounds of food a day. It spends about 18 hours each day just looking for that much. *Seismosaurus*, about 20 times heavier than an elephant, must have eaten a lot! Paleontologists still aren't sure how it found time to forage for all that food.

The smallest dinosaur paleontologists have found was probably the little meat eater *Compsognathus*. It was about 35 inches long and weighed only about five pounds. One *Compsognathus* was so well preserved in limestone that paleontologists could make out the bones of an iguana-like lizard in its stomach.

In one way eating plants is easier than eating meat: Plants don't run away. But plants are harder to digest than meat is. So, the herbivores needed larger digestive systems. That is one reason they became so big. Too heavy to balance on their hind legs, most of the big plant eaters walked on all fours.

Dinosaurs either ate plants or other animals. The plant eaters (herbivores) probably outnumbered the meat eaters (carnivores) by 20 to 1.

Plant eaters had to protect themselves from carnivores. Some, like these *Triceratops*, protected themselves with body armor and defensive weapons such as horns.

Other dinosaurs had dangerous, spiked clubs on the ends of their tails. They used these weapons to fend off attackers.

Most meat-eating dinosaurs were equipped with powerful jaws, sharp, flesh-tearing teeth, and strong legs for chasing or leaping out at prey.

The most famous and largest of the predators is *Tyrannosaurus*. It probably preyed mostly on dinosaurs that traveled in herds. The word dinosaur means "terrible lizard" and *Tyrannosaurus* was truly a terrifying creature.

Old-theory
Tyrannosaurus

For a long time paleontologists pictured *Tyrannosaurus* in an upright position with its tail dragging on the ground behind it for support. Today, most scientists agree that *Tyrannosaurus* probably kept its tail off the ground. It used its tail to help keep its balance since its huge, powerful head was so heavy.

New-theory
Tyrannosaurus

Another meat eater was *Spinosaurus*. Like Tyran-
nosaurus it was about 40 feet long, but it lived in what is now
northern Africa. Its strangest feature was a big piece of skin that looked
like a sail on its back. Scientists aren't sure what it used this for. Maybe *Spinosaurus*
used it to attract the attention of mates who were far away. If that was the case, it
was probably brightly colored like it is here. Other paleontologists think the "sail"
was used to regulate the dinosaur's body temperature. On hot days *Spinosaurus* would
have caught cool breezes in the sail to cool its blood. On cool days it would have
put its sail in the sun to warm itself.

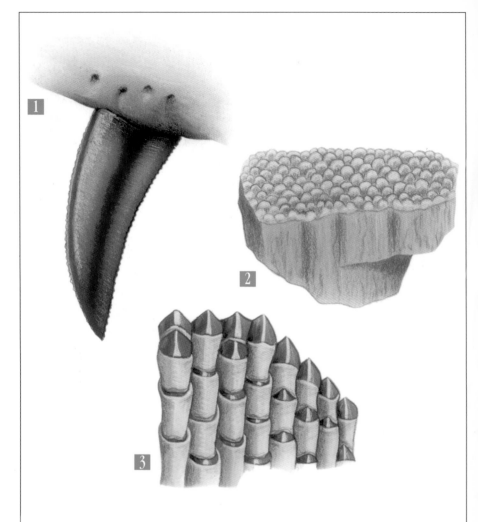

From looking at fossils of dinosaur jaws paleontologists can tell that dinosaurs constantly grew new teeth. When old ones broke off or wore down, new ones would replace them.

Dinosaur teeth tell paleontologists a lot about the animals they came from.

1. *Tyrannosaurus* tooth with knife-like edge for tearing flesh
2. *Trachodon* tooth with flat grinding surface for breaking down twigs and leaves
3. *Iguanodon* tooth for grinding plants. *Iguanodon* would pluck vegetation off of trees with a horny beak at the front of its jaws. Then it would chew thoroughly with grinders in the back of its mouth before swallowing.

Stegosaurus, above, had a very small brain. It only weighed about two and a half ounces and was the size of a ping-pong ball. That's pretty amazing since *Stegosaurus* weighed about two tons.

But modern reptiles have equally small brains compared to their body size and they've survived hundreds of millions of years, too.

Troodon, from Late Cretaceous Canada, was a small meat-eater and had a brain about the size of some of today's birds. It's brain-to-body ratio suggests that it may have been the most intelligent dinosaur, though most of its brain was probably devoted to its senses.

Archaeopteryx is the first bird we know of. It is sometimes called a "feathered dinosaur" because its skeleton looks a lot like those of other dinosaurs in the late Jurassic. But unlike other dinosaurs, *Archaeopteryx* had feathers. It may have shared an ancestor with modern birds.

A lot of people think all of the dinosaurs became extinct at the end of the Cretaceous. In fact, there are about 9,000 species alive today. They are called birds.

Birds are dinosaurs?

In a sense, yes. Today's birds had dinosaur ancestors.

At the end of the Cretaceous, about 150 years after the first dinosaurs appeared, nearly all of them became extinct. Scientists still don't know for sure just what killed them. There seems to have been a big and relatively fast change in the Earth's weather. Climate change may have been caused by all the geological activity going on at that time: continental drift, the rise of mountains, volcanic eruptions, and widespread sea-level changes.

Another theory is that mammals came to be so good at eating dinosaur eggs that they ate the dinosaurs out of existence.

Many scientists believe climate change in the Cretaceous was caused by a huge asteroid that hit the Earth about 65 million years ago. They say it was so big and hit so hard that it sent great clouds of dust into the air, blocking plants from the sunlight they need to live. Without plants the herbivores would soon have died of starvation. And without herbivores to eat, the carnivores would soon have followed.

But this theory of mass dinosaur extinction doesn't satisfy everyone. If it was an asteroid, some scientists ask, then why didn't it also kill the mammals that have survived until today? Maybe because mammals were warm-blooded and could better adapt to cooling temperatures, other scientists answer.

Then where does that leave birds? No one yet knows for sure.

There are still lots of unanswered questions
about the lives and deaths of the dinosaurs.
There is still a lot of work for
paleontologists to do.

Paleontology Department

STAFF ONLY

DO NOT ENTER

Maybe we can
come back *later!*

It may take a few million
years for the dust to settle.

Glossary

Age of Dinosaurs: period between 243 and 65 million years ago when dinosaurs were common

asteroid: chunk of matter that comes to Earth from beyond Earth's atmosphere

bacteria: microscopic single-cell creatures

carnivore: flesh-eating animal

cartilage: strong, flexible tissue

conodonts: common ancestors of all dinosaurs as well as modern birds and crocodiles

Cretaceous Period: third and final part of the Age of Dinosaurs from 146 to 65 million years ago

extinction: death of every individual of a species

herbivore: animal that eats only plants

Jurassic Period: the second part of the Age of Dinosaurs from 208 to 146 million years ago.

microscopic: too small to see without a microscope

natural selection: process where success of a well-adapted life form leads to continuation of its traits in subsequent generations

paleontologist: scientist who studies fossils to learn about life in the past

Pangaea: huge land mass of all modern continents, began to break up 135 million years ago

predator: animal that hunts and eats other animals

prey: animal hunted and eaten by a predator

pterosaurs: flying reptiles related to dinosaurs

Quaternary Period: the current geological period, beginning 1.2 million years ago

sauropods: large, long-necked, herbivorous dinosaurs

species: creatures of a particular type

thecodonts: mixed group of reptiles including the ancestors of dinosaurs, crocodiles, and pterosaurs

Triassic Period: the first part of the Age of Dinosaurs from 243 to 208 million years ago

vertebrates: animals with backbones